and the Snowy Day

by Claudia Carlson and Ann D. Koffsky
illustrations by CB Decker

Inspired by Jacqueline Goldman and her longtime vision to produce a children's book about the miraculous, lifesaving work of Magen David Adom.

Springfield, NJ · Jerusalem

With gratitude to Claudia for bringing Avi to life.
—ADK and CBD

Apples & Honey Press
An imprint of Behrman House and Gefen Publishing House
Behrman House, 11 Edison Place, Springfield, New Jersey 07081
Gefen Publishing House Ltd., 6 Hatzvi Street, Jerusalem, 94386, Israel
www.applesandhoneypress.com

Copyright © 2017 by American Friends of Magen David Adom
ISBN: 978-1-68115-528-9
All rights reserved. No part of this publication may be translated, reproduced, stored in a retrieval system, or transmitted, in any form or by an means, electronic, mechanical, photocopying, recording, or otherwise, without express written permission from the publishers. The characters in this book are under trademark by American Friends of Magen David Adom.

The publisher gratefully acknowledges the following sources of photographs: P. 32 Shutterstock: Kislitsin Dmitrii (bandage); S1001 (hospital); Alexandra Lande (Jerusalem); chainarong06 (hands); Kozlenko (snow chains); Arina P Habich (snowstorm); ChameleonsEye (Tel Aviv); Syda Productions (z'rizut). All other photos used by permission from Magen David Adom.

Library of Congress Cataloging-in-Publication Data
Names: Carlson, Claudia, author. | Koffsky, Ann D., author. | Decker, C. B., illustrator.
Title: Avi the ambulance and the snowy day / by Claudia Carlson and Ann D. Koffsky ; illustrated by CB Decker.
Description: Springfield, NJ : Apples & Honey Press, [2017] |
Summary: "Avi the Ambulance helps people in Jerusalem during a snowstorm"—Provided by publisher.
Identifiers: LCCN 2016014954 | ISBN 9781681155289
Subjects: | CYAC: Ambulances—Fiction. | Emergency vehicles—Fiction. | Rescue work—Fiction. | Snow—Fiction. | Jews—Israel—Fiction. | Israel—Fiction.
Classification: LCC PZ7.1.C4 Ar 2017 | DDC [E]--dc23 LC record available at https://lccn.loc.gov/2016014954

Edited by Dena Neusner
Art Directed by Ann D. Koffsky
Design by David Neuhaus
Printed in China

1 3 5 7 9 8 6 4 2

0422/B1859/A3

In a garage in Jerusalem lived a family of ambulances. They all worked together to help save lives.

MAGEN DAVID ADOM IN ISRAEL
מגן דוד אדום בישראל

Sometimes they had fun together, too.

"Avi! Come outside!" called Avi's sister, Maya, with a laugh. "It's snowing!"

It hardly ever snows in Jerusalem, so Avi quickly rolled out to see.

Squish! Maya hit his grill with a snowball.

"I'll get you for that!" called Avi, and he started collecting snow.

Squash! Hila the helicopter's snowball hit Maya right on her light bar.

Soon snowballs were flying everywhere!

"Okay, okay, you've all had your fun," said Avi's mom with a smile, "but we have to clear the ice and snow. If there are any emergencies, we'll need to be able to drive out fast, without sliding and skidding."

Zack and Leah began shoveling the snow, while Maya and Avi made sure no ice had formed on the driveway. Soon, the path was clear.

Just then, a call came in. *Ring, ring!*

"There's been an accident on the highway to Tel Aviv," called Avi's father. "Avi and Zack—go and see if you can help!"

Zack threw down his snow shovel and hopped into Avi. They raced down the now-clean driveway.

"No slipping and sliding!" Avi said.

"Let's drive fast!" said Zack.

They sped toward Tel Aviv, up one hill, and down the next with no problem. But just as they started to climb the third hill, the snow began to fall faster. Avi's windshield wipers couldn't keep up, and Zack was having trouble seeing the road ahead.

Who-oooaaaa

"Whoa is right! We'd better slow down," said Zack. "We won't be able to help if we get in an accident, too."

So Avi continued much more slowly along the Jerusalem-to-Tel Aviv highway, with his lights on their brightest.

Finally, Avi and Zack reached the accident. It was a pileup! Three cars had spun and slid into one another. Taillights were shattered, bumpers were dented, and the cars were stuck in snowdrifts. No one could get anywhere at all!

"Is everyone okay?" asked Avi.

"We're okay," answered an older man, "but I banged up my leg. And my car can't move!"

“We’re stuck too!” said a man from the middle car. “And my friend bumped his head when we crashed.”

“I’m really c-c-c-cold,” said a young girl, shivering.

"Zack, please get blankets and bandages from my storage compartment and share them with everyone who needs them," Avi said.

Soon everyone was feeling much better.

But they were still stuck. Avi didn't know what to do. The snow was even deeper now, and when he tried to drive through it, his tires spun around and around, but he stayed right where he was. Usually he and Zack helped people by bringing them to the hospital, where they could get the care they needed.

But how were they going to bring anyone anywhere if Avi couldn't move?

Just then, he heard a faint sound. *Woo! Wooo!*

It was getting louder. *WOO! WOOO!*

He and Zack squinted through the swirling snow.

They could see red and white lights shining . . .
then a big yellow blob. . . . It was Maya!

"Need some help, little brother?" Maya asked as she pulled up.

"I'm not so little!" Avi protested. "But yes, we sure do!"

"Here. We brought you a set of snow chains like mine," said Leah, Maya's medic.

"Avi, you really should have brought yours with you before rushing out into the snow!" Maya scolded. "You are an ambulance. You need to always be prepared!"

"You're right," said Avi, feeling ashamed. "It won't happen again. I promise."

"Okay. I know you'll remember from now on. Put them on your tires, and let's work together to take anyone who needs help to the hospital. A tow truck is on its way to help, too."

Soon, the snow chains were on, and Zack and Leah helped the people who were hurt climb aboard Avi and Maya.

Once they were safely inside, Maya and Avi started driving. Whew! Now Avi's tires worked the way they should.

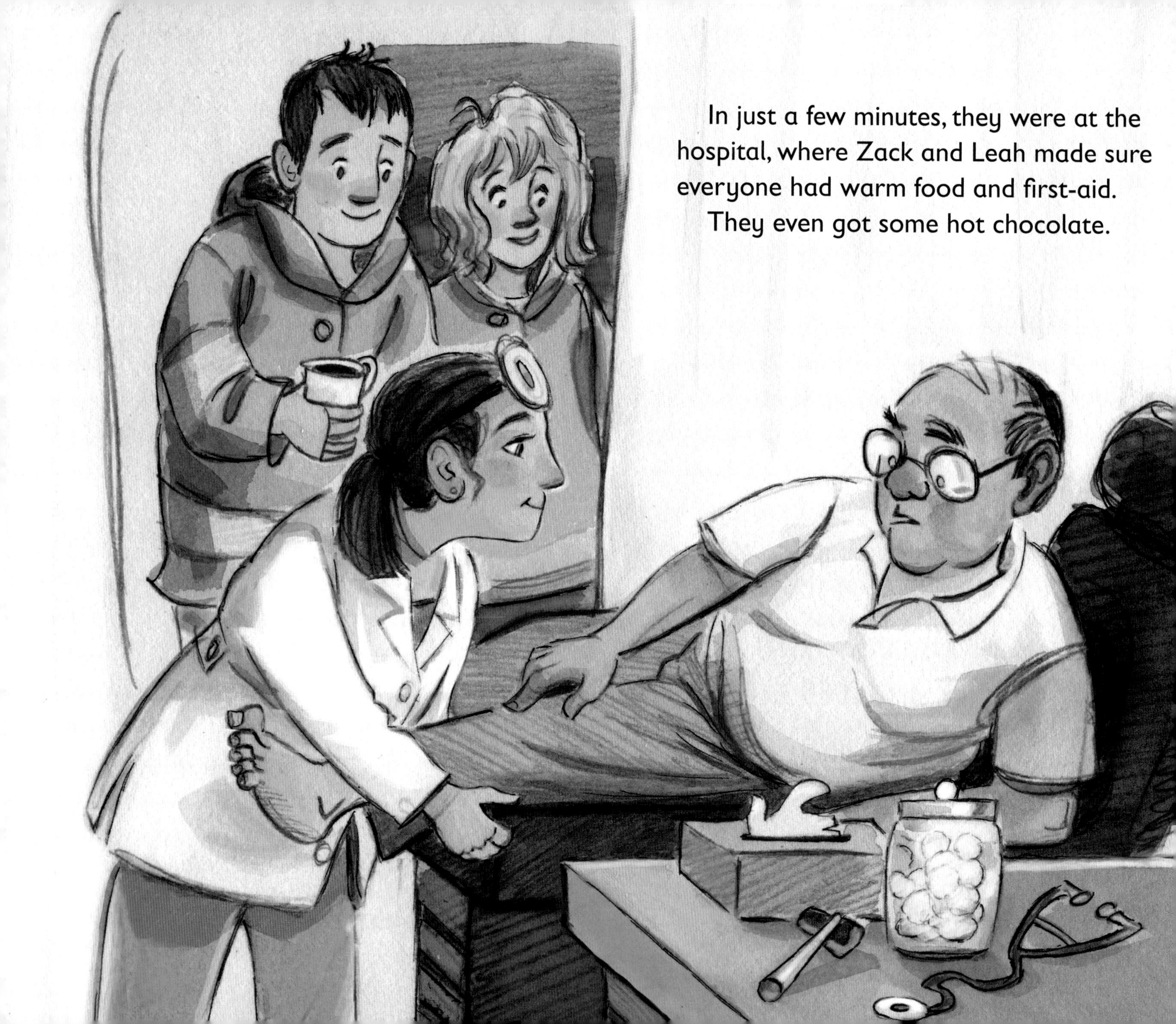

In just a few minutes, they were at the hospital, where Zack and Leah made sure everyone had warm food and first-aid.

They even got some hot chocolate.

Once everyone was comfortable, Avi and Maya headed back to the garage.

"Wow," said Avi. "I can't remember it ever snowing like this in Jerusalem before!"

"I know! It's so pretty. I love the snow—Hey!"

"I told you before I'd get you back!" Avi grinned.

The Lifesaving Work of Magen David Adom

Avi the Ambulance and the Snowy Day is based on the real work of Magen David Adom, Israel's ambulance, blood-services, and disaster-relief organization, whose emergency medical first responders serve the country's more than eight million people. The story highlights Jewish values such as *piku'ach nefesh*, the importance of saving lives, and *g'vurah*, heroism.

More than fourteen thousand professionals and volunteers help save lives at MDA. You can learn more at www.afmda.org.

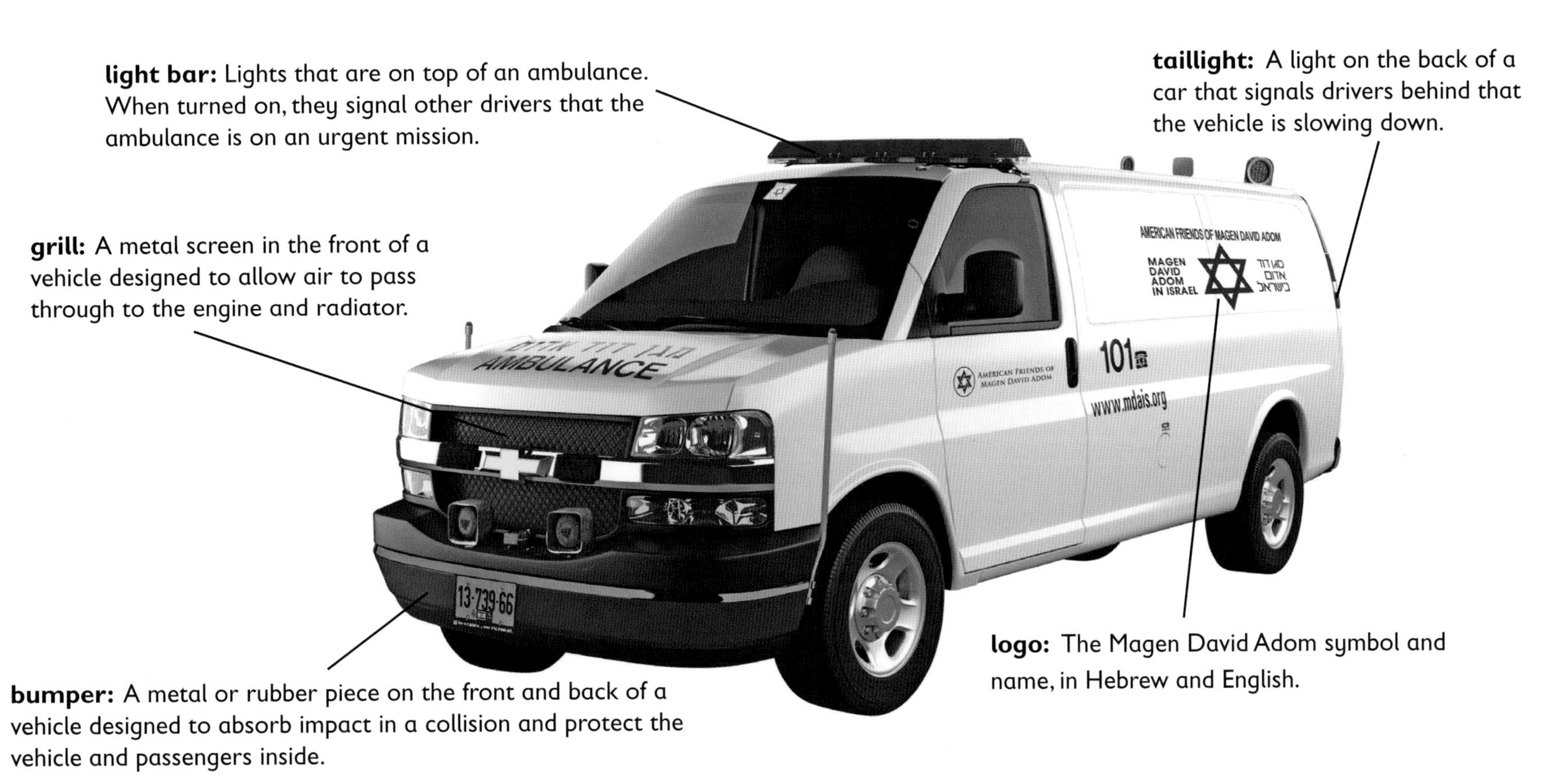

Vocabulary

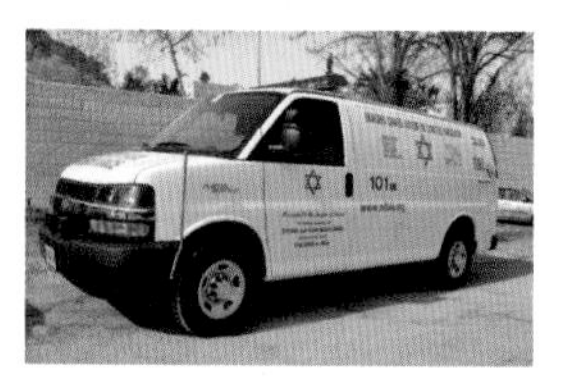

ambulance: A special truck used to move hurt or sick people to a hospital. Avi is an ambulance.

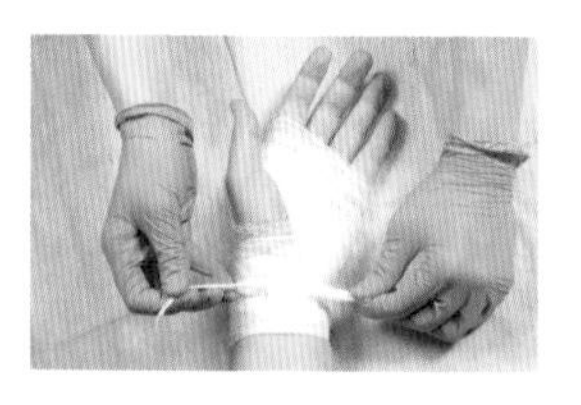

bandage: A piece of material used to protect an injured part of the body.

***g'vurah*:** Heroism. Jewish tradition challenges us to stand up, be brave, and do what is good for humanity.

hospital: A building where doctors, nurses, and others take care of hurt and sick people. (*pictured: Hadassah Ein Kerem Hospital*)

Jerusalem: The capital city of Israel. Jerusalem is one of the oldest cities in the world.

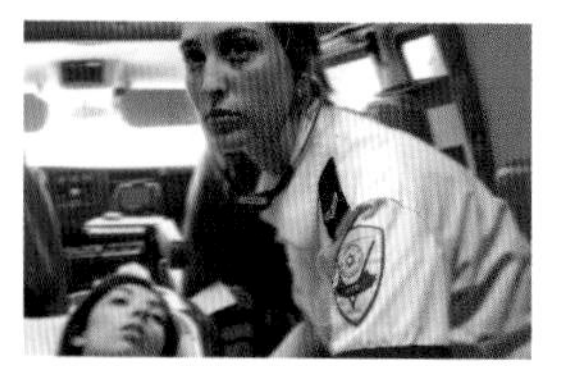

medic: A person trained to help take care of hurt or sick people. Zack and Leah are medics.

mobile intensive care unit (MICU): A bigger ambulance that has more medical supplies to take care of people who are very hurt or sick. Maya is a MICU.

piku'ach nefesh: The Jewish value of saving a life. *Piku'ach nefesh* is so important, it supersedes virtually every other commandment in the Torah.

snow chains: Metal chains that are fitted around a vehicle's tires to help give it mobility and extra traction in the snow.

snowstorm: A storm where large amounts of snow falls. A snowstorm can often cause difficult road conditions, including slick roads and poor visibility. This is particularly true in Israel, where snowfall is very rare, and many people are unprepared for it.

Tel Aviv: The second largest city in Israel. Tel Aviv is a business hub and cultural center.

***z'rizut*:** The Jewish value of contributing to society enthusiastically and swiftly.